For Levi
Because you're never too old for bunnies

tiger tales
5 River Road, Suite 128, Wilton, CT 06897
Published in the United States 2016
Originally published in Great Britain 2016
by Little Tiger Press
Text and illustrations copyright © 2016 Tim Warnes
Visit Tim Warnes at www.ChapmanandWarnes.com
ISBN-13: 978-1-68010-013-6
ISBN-10: 1-68010-013-0
Printed in China
LTP/1400/1250/0915
10 9 8 7 6 5 4 3 2 1

For more insight and activities, visit us at
www.tigertalesbooks.com

Missing Hat
Do not touch!
If found, contact
THE GREAT RENATO
IMMEDIATELY

reed

dragonfly

friend

WARNING!
DO NOT TOUCH!

by tim

warnes

tiger  tales

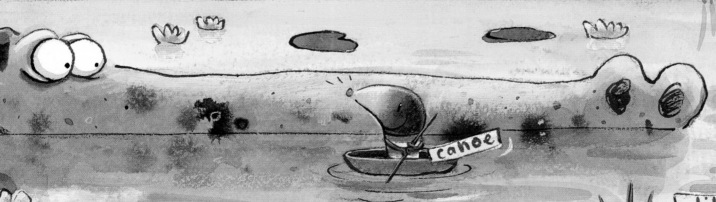

canoe

lily pad

lily

Mole loved labeling things.

All kinds of things.

Anything, really.

It was his absolute favorite thing to do.

His best friend, the Lumpy-Bumpy Thing,

was pretty good at it, too.

One day, the two friends saw something unusual in the woods.

"**Look!**" gasped Mole. "A **snow bunny!** I've seen **brown** bunnies and **black** bunnies and **gray** bunnies before, but I've never seen a white one."

It was very mysterious indeed.

Mole started to label the bunny. But it bounced away.

"Stop that bunny!" cried Mole.

So the Lumpy-Bumpy Thing chased after it.

The Lumpy-Bumpy Thing came back
wearing an interesting-looking hat.
The hat already had a label:
WARNING! Do not touch!

"Quick! Take it off!"
cried Mole. "It could be dangerous!"

But the Lumpy-Bumpy Thing just giggled. Then it lifted up the hat.

WARNING! Do not touch!

There, on its head, was another bunny, with a very **tickly** tail. **"Unbelievable!"** gasped Mole. **"That hat's magic!"**

The bunny jumped down and gave Mole a great big snuggle.

"I suppose it's safe enough," Mole grinned. "After all, they ARE just bunnies."

On-off, on-off went the magic hat.

"Look how many bunnies you've made!" exclaimed Mole. "I'm going to number them so we can play Bunny Bingo!"

The Lumpy-Bumpy Thing was in Bunny Heaven!

But Mole was not. Those **naughty** bunnies kept swapping places and mixing themselves up.

It was all **very confusing.**

"Ten, seven, nine, five—wait! That's not right,"
grumbled Mole. "Hold still!"
But the bunnies wouldn't listen.

Bunny after bunny
jumped out of the hat.

"97, 98, 99, 100!"

What had started
out as a little bit of fun
quickly became a
big problem.

"Make it STOP!" hollered Mole.

The Lumpy-Bumpy Thing tried pushing the bunnies back into the hat. But they were too wriggly.

It tried scaring them away. But they weren't scared at all.

"Look at this mess!" wailed Mole.
The bunnies had eaten all the flowers.
And they'd dug hundreds of holes.

"Stop it!
Bad bunnies!"
cried Mole.

Then the Lumpy-Bumpy Thing spotted something terrible!

Number 54 was heading straight for Mole's vegetable garden . . . .

Mole ran after him.
"Give me that carrot!"
he demanded.

They tugged and they pulled,

and they pulled and they tugged, until . . .

Oof!

Number 54 let go.

"Ha ha! Got it!" shouted Mole, waving the carrot triumphantly in the air.
The other bunnies stopped and stared and twitched their noses . . .

"RUN FOR IT!"

yelled Mole.

But the Lumpy-Bumpy Thing stumbled.
Mole's carrot sailed through the air . . .

. . . and fell with a **plop!** into the magic hat.

One of the bunnies dived in after it . . . and disappeared!

"Hooray!" cried Mole. "Quick! Grab some more carrots!"

So the two friends started hurling them into the hat. And one by one, the bunnies followed.

"Ten, nine, eight, seven, six, five, four, three, two, one, ZERO BUNNIES!" declared Mole. "We did it!"

The Lumpy-Bumpy Thing
peered nervously
into the hat.
    "Don't worry," said Mole.
"They're gone now."

Very carefully,
they carried it back to
where they'd found it.

"We don't want any more trouble, do we?" said Mole.

But the Lumpy-Bumpy Thing was looking at something unusual in the grass—something with a label on it.

"Don't touch that!" gulped Mole.

But it was too late . . . .

"Oh, no!" cried Mole.
"Not again!"